A Dad's Delight

written and illustrated by

Janet Willis

The Khesed Foundation
NASHVILLE, TENNESSEE

Thank you Rich Kryczka
American Academy of Art, Chicago

www.adadsdelight.org

Scripture quotation is from the New International Version
with capitalizations added
ISBN 0-9785077-0-3 ISBN 0-9785077-1-1 (pbk.)
SAN: 850-7236

Printed in the United States of America
by Lithographics Inc.

to

	P
Amy	3B
Toby	C
Dan	LF
Ben	CF
Joe	1B
Sam	2B
Hank	RF
Elizabeth	SS
Pete	

Hank loved baseball

and Dad loved Hank.

It all started early one morning,

right off the bat.

"Hank Boston!" Dad named his new son
even though they lived in Chicago.

"Now what's his real name?"
Grandma asked. But this was
one time Dad wasn't kidding.

As little Hank grew, Dad explained, "When I was a young baseball fan, my hero played for the Boston Red Sox. He was the greatest hitter who ever lived."

When Hank was three
and a-half, he drew a
picture of himself making sure
to put a "B" on his cap.
"That's for Boston!"
he told everyone.

Dad made time for his boys. "Who wants to play catch?" he often called.

"I do!" rang out all over the house as each boy grabbed his cap and mitt and dashed after Dad.

When Dad was at work, the boys played wiffleball for hours in their small backyard.

"Whack!"
went the bat.
"I've got it!" Sam called.
"Way to go!" Hank yelled
as Sam made a diving catch.

When Hank turned six, his family moved to a new place in Chicago where he got his big chance. The older boys were all on Little League teams, but Sam's team needed another player.
"I've got a little brother," Sam said.

So Hank was in...

uniform and all!

Sometimes he played short
center or even second
base, but what he
really wanted
to do was
pitch.

One game Hank begged, "Coach, we're way ahead. Please Coach, please can I pitch...please?" Finally Coach said, "OK."

"Hmm," Hank whispered to himself, "I remember Dad showed us that old-time baseball movie.

Maybe I'll try that old-time pitch."

He spun his arm around,
and around, and
around,
then...

let it fly!

"Dad! Dad! Did you see that?
Two innings and I didn't give
up a run!" Hank beamed.

The next day
Hank was excited!

His pitching career was off to a great start.
He jumped out of bed, gobbled down his
breakfast, and hurried through his chores.
"Everybody is busy so I'll just
practice by myself,"
Hank said as he
went outside.

Now his family
had moved to a new
second floor apartment
and Hank eyed the big brick
wall right next to Dad's downstairs office.
"That's a perfect spot for pitching practice!"   Hank said.

NO
BALLPLAYING
NEAR THE
BUILDING

Then he read the rule
posted in the window
"Oh, just this once.
I'll be really careful,"
he decided.

Suddenly upstairs
Mom heard,

CRASH!

clinkle

clink!

Mom met her boy
as he came slowly
up the stairs.   "Hank,
this is pretty serious,"
she said.   "You'll have to
wait 'till Dad comes home."

Hank waited at his bedroom window all afternoon.
He gazed down the street, took a deep breath, and sighed to himself,
"This is the longest day of my life."   Finally, the van pulled up.

Dad had no trouble
figuring out the culprit.

"I'm in big trouble now,"
Hank said softly as
he followed Dad
downstairs
to the
office.

"I know I broke the rule,
Dad," Hank admitted,
"and I'm really sorry."

"That's good,
    but Hank there's still a problem,"
Dad answered.   "Someone
    is going to have to pay
        for this window."

Dad thought for a minute,
put his arm around Hank,
then continued, "I know
I've broken some rules myself, Hank.
And even though I was sorry,
I learned a penalty eventually
would have to be paid."

"But there was Someone who didn't want me to have to pay, so He paid it for me."

"Oh, I know who that was--Jesus!" Hank said.

Dad slowly nodded, "He is the greatest hero of all." Then Hank watched as Dad bent down, found the ball, and carefully brushed off the broken glass. "I'll pay for the window, Hank. Just sign the ball."

And Dad
put it up
on his bookshelf.

Hank learned
an important
lesson
that day...

a lesson about
a father's mercy.

And
more than
that, Hank learned...

giving mercy
was Dad's delight.

"Who is a God like You,
Who pardons sin...
You do not stay angry forever,
but delight
to show mercy."
Micah 7:18

This is a true story.
The names and places
have not been changed
to protect the guilty...

because the guilty
are guilty no more!